How to Zap Zombies

To make sure they stay away for good,
you have to destroy zombies twice.
That way they're no longer the living-dead:

They're dead-dead.

And to make sure the dead-deads are really, really dead,
it's best to read this book again!

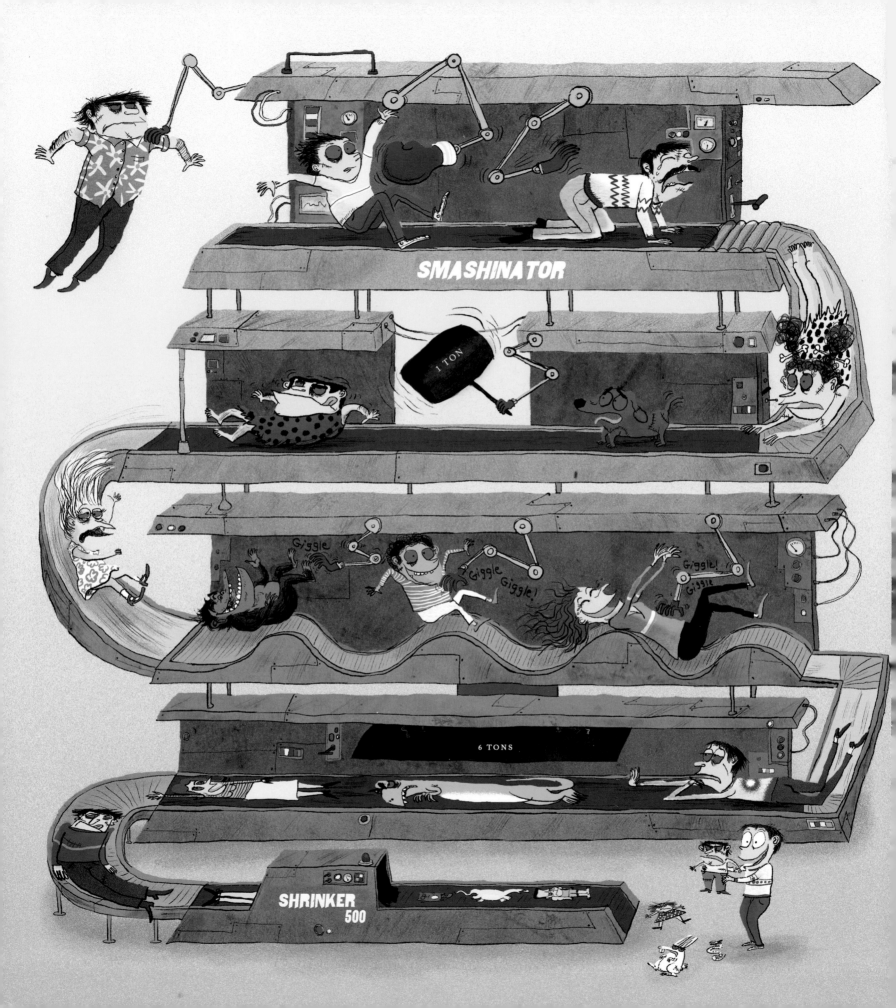

Some zombies come from very far away . . .
They march slowly like cavemen,
dressed in animal prints, and the scariest ones
are **real animals**!

There are some zombies who are lost:
They don't know what they're doing or where they're going.
Try to **trap them** inside the zombie zoo.

But **don't forget** to take off your disguise
before going to school or going home . . .

Zombies are even scarier
when they show up in large groups.
But you can trick the enemy:

Dress up like a
ZOMBIE
to blend in!

You're better off pretending you're already sick.

Some of them want to bite us and turn us into zombies, too.

Some zombies like to wear silly hats.
They walk around with soda bottles
on their way to creepy zombie parties.
So take away their favorite things!

That will **confuse them** and
stop them from causing trouble.

Penny-pinching zombies can't resist money.

Dangle a coin just out of reach,
to keep them **hypnotized**.

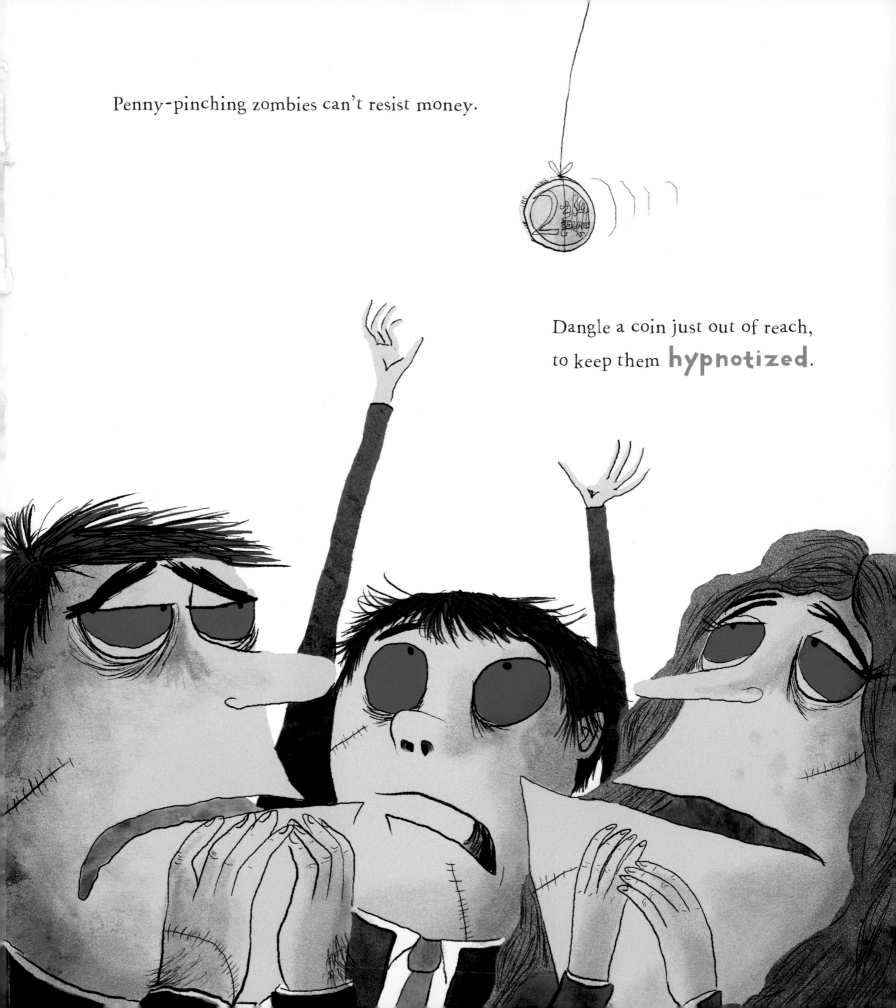

Zombies who wear kilts like to play the bagpipe.

Carefully plug up the ends of their pipes:
They will blow really hard and **explode**!

Zombies have weak spots.
Some zombies can't see without their glasses.
Just hose them down and **blind them**!

Zombies do not speak, and they walk very slowly,
with their arms straight out or dangling at their sides.
All you have to do is **run away**. They won't be able to catch up to you!

Zombie gorilla

Zombie vegetables

Zombie Martian

Zombie princess

Zombie dragon

Dummy, not a zombie

Like the vegetables they resemble, they have spent a lot of time underground.
But just because someone looks like a dummy doesn't mean they're a zombie!

Zombie

Frankenstein zombie

Giant zombie

Zombie rabbit

Zombie mummy

Little zombie girl

Make sure you know how to recognize zombies: Their skin is wrinkly like a potato, their eyes are tomato **red**, and their mouths are the color of **beets**.

Brain protector

Bow and
poison arrows

Magic broom

Super zapper
spaceship

Shield

Hypnotic dress

Butt-kicking
boots

BEWARE!

This is not a book for babies. . . .
It's only meant for the brave boys and girls
who dare to face down scary zombies!

Sturdy helmet

Sticky dart gun

Star badge
for courage

Zombie rake

Epic sword

Superhero cape

How to Zap Zombies

Catherine Leblanc   Roland Garrigue

INSIGHT KIDS

San Rafael, California

The End

To my courageous little kids!
C.L.

I dedicate this book to Thomas, Marie, Rémi, Hugo,
Lucie, Louis, Alexandre, Simon, and Anna-lou . . .
my list of nieces and nephews keeps growing!
R.G.

INSIGHT
KIDS

PO Box 3088
San Rafael, CA 94912
www.insighteditions.com

Find us on Facebook: www.facebook.com/InsightEditions
Follow us on Twitter: @insighteditions

First published in the United States in 2014 by Insight Editions.
Originally published in France in 2013 by Éditions Glénat as
Comment Ratatiner les Zombies?
by C. Leblanc and R. Garrigue.
© 2013 Éditions Glénat
Translation © 2014 Insight Editions

Thanks to Christopher Goff and Marie Goff-Tuttle
for their help in translating this book.

Library of Congress Cataloging-in-Publication Data available.

ISBN: 978-1-60887-442-2

ROOTS of PEACE   REPLANTED PAPER

Insight Editions, in association with Roots of Peace, will plant two trees for each tree used in the
manufacturing of this book. Roots of Peace is an internationally renowned humanitarian organization
dedicated to eradicating land mines worldwide and converting war-torn lands into productive farms
and wildlife habitats. Roots of Peace will plant two million fruit and nut trees in Afghanistan and
provide farmers there with the skills and support necessary for sustainable land use.

Manufactured in China by Insight Editions

10 9 8 7 6 5 4 3 2 1